4th edition

NEW!
MUSIC THEORY
for Young Musicians

gr **2**

🐝 A thorough preparation for **ABRSM Online Theory Exams**
🐝 A step by step walk-through with explanations, examples, tips, exercises and revision

Name
_____

Phone
_____

YING YING NG

pocostudio
MAKE SENSE OF MUSIC

Welcome to Poco Music Theory

Valuable to those who prefer a step by step, innovative approach, this series is designed to give students the opportunity to achieve well and enjoy their learning. It provides engaging activities to develop strong music literacy skills.

The fourth edition was motivated by two main drivers, external and internal. The external landscape has changed: in response to the Covid pandemic, ABRSM has moved the assessment of Music Theory to an online exam. Internally, there is always a need to look at how we can improve the current structure.

Building on past successes and coping with future challenges, this new edition follows four principles that are dear to our hearts:

- **comprehensiveness**, offering comprehensive coverage of the syllabus for ABRSM exams;

 An exam question format.

- **simplification**, breaking down musical concepts into smaller, simpler components;

A visual tip shows a simpler way to understand a concept.

- **accessibility**, providing a step by step walk-through ABRSM exam style questions.

 A guide to tackle an exam question.

 An example.

 Sing, Play, and Compose Music game reference.

 Poco Keyboard Flashcards game reference.

 A rhythmic practice.

- **student-centred approach**, working from simple to complex progressively, one step at a time using simple, logical language, creative visual aids, and uncluttered, attractive format to increase the student's understanding of the topic.

 A note supplies explanations.

I hope students and teachers will enjoy using these books, and I wish them every success.

Ying Ying Ng

Contents

1 **Pitch 1**
Ledger lines: Bass clef notes
Ledger lines: Treble clef notes
Notes at the same pitch in treble and bass clefs
4

2 **Rhythm 1**
Time names and time values
Dotted notes
Time signatures
Rewriting rhythms in different metres
10

3 **Rhythm 2**
Triplets
Grouping notes by beat
Grouping notes across multiple beats
Grouping rests
19

4 **Keys and Scales**
The major scales of A, B♭ and E♭
Circle of 5ths: Major keys
Relative majors and minors
The minor scales of A, E and D
28

5 **Intervals**
Intervals in major and minor scales
44

6 **Tonic Triads**
Tonic triads in major and minor keys
48

7 **Terms and Signs**
Tempo
Dynamics
Expression
General
Articulation
Musical signs
Musical terms
52

8 **Music in Context**
62

9 **Model Test Paper**
66

10 **Quick Revision**
74

Ledger lines: Bass clef notes
Ledger lines: Treble clef notes
Notes at the same pitch in treble and bass clefs

1 Pitch 1

Ledger lines: Bass clef notes

• A ledger line is a short line added above or below the stave (staff) to extend its range.

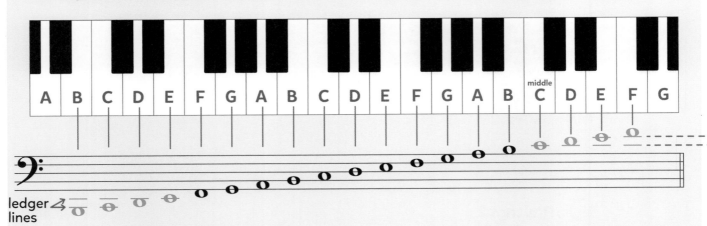

1 Trace and copy the ledger notes and note names.

E D C B

C D E F

2 Fill in the missing notes as semibreves (whole notes). Write the note names.

(a)

(b)

3 Write the note names.

(a)

(b)

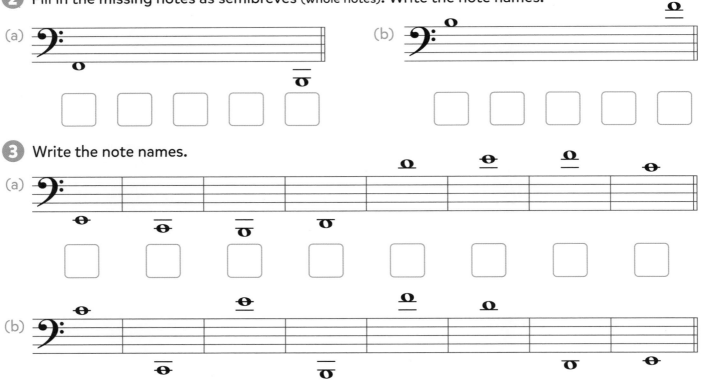

Ledger lines: Treble clef notes

4 Trace and copy the ledger notes and note names.

C B A G

A B C D

5 Fill in the missing notes as semibreves (whole notes). Write the note names.

(a)

(b)

6 Write the note names.

(a)

(b)

7 Tick ☑ the correct note name. EXAM

(a)
F	G	A	B
☐	☐	☐	☐

(b)
C#	D#	F#	G#
☐	☐	☐	☐

(c)
E	C	E♭	B♭
☐	☐	☐	☐

(d)
B♭	E♭	A♭	A
☐	☐	☐	☐

(e)
A	E	C	F
☐	☐	☐	☐

(f)
C#	D#	F#	G#
☐	☐	☐	☐

8 Add the correct clef.

B   E♭   G#   D   C#   A

9 Tick ☑ the correct clef. EXAM

(a) D#   𝄞 ☐ 𝄢 ☐

(b) E   𝄞 ☐ 𝄢 ☐

(c) B♭   𝄞 ☐ 𝄢 ☐

(d) A#   𝄞 ☐ 𝄢 ☐

(e) D#   𝄞 ☐ 𝄢 ☐

(f) A   𝄞 ☐ 𝄢 ☐

(g) G♭   𝄞 ☐ 𝄢 ☐

(h) E♭   𝄞 ☐ 𝄢 ☐

Notes at the same pitch in treble and bass clefs

10 Rewrite the notes in the new clef, keeping the same pitch.

(a)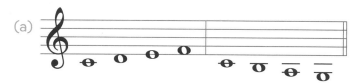

(b)

EXAM

❶ Write middle C for each clef as a guide.
❷ Find out if the note is above/below middle C.

(c)

(d)

(e)

(f)

(g)

(h)

(i)

(j)

(k)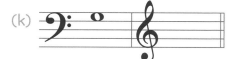

(l)

(m)

(n)

11 Tick ☑ or cross ☒ to show if the notes are at the same pitch.

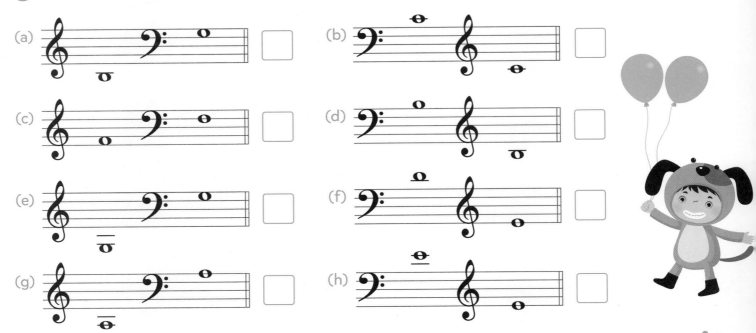

(a) ☐

(b) ☐

(c) ☐

(d) ☐

(e) ☐

(f) ☐

(g) ☐

(h) ☐

12 Circle if the second note is **lower, higher** or the **same** as the first note.

> ① Write middle C for each clef as a guide.
> ② Name notes.
> ③ Compare notes.

(a)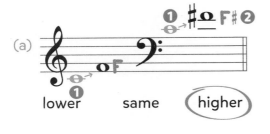

lower   same   (higher)

(b)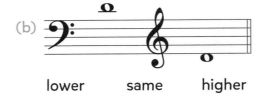

lower   same   higher

(c)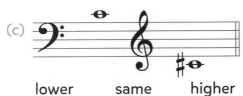

lower   same   higher

(d)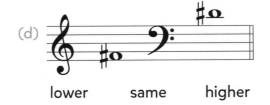

lower   same   higher

(e)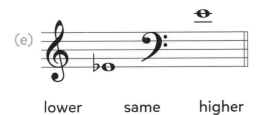

lower   same   higher

(f)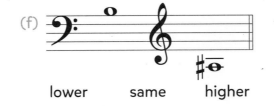

lower   same   higher

(g)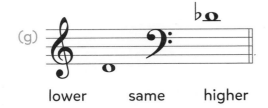

lower   same   higher

(h)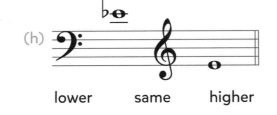

lower   same   higher

13 Circle **TRUE** or **FALSE**. EXAM

❶ Underline keywords.
❷ Name notes.
❸ Indicate if 2nd note is higher/lower.
❹ Verify statement.

(a)  The first note sounds **higher** than the second note.   ❹ TRUE (FALSE)

(b)  The second note sounds **lower** than the first note.   TRUE   FALSE

(c)  The first note sounds **lower** than the second note.   TRUE   FALSE

(d)  The second note sounds **higher** than the first note.   TRUE   FALSE

(e)  The first note sounds **higher** than the second note.   TRUE   FALSE

(f)  The second note sounds **lower** than the first note.   TRUE   FALSE

(g)  The first note sounds **higher** than the second note.   TRUE   FALSE

(h)  The second note sounds **higher** than the first note.   TRUE   FALSE

Time names and time values
Dotted notes, Time signatures
Rewriting rhythms in different metres

② Rhythm 1

Time names and time values

	Time name	Note	Rest	Time value
longest	**semibreve** (whole note)	𝅝	▬	4 × 𝅘𝅥
	minim (half note)	𝅗𝅥	▬	2 × 𝅘𝅥
	crotchet (quarter note)	𝅘𝅥	𝄽	1 × 𝅘𝅥
	quaver (8th note)	𝅘𝅥𝅮	𝄾	$\frac{1}{2}$ × 𝅘𝅥
shortest	**semiquaver** (16th note)	𝅘𝅥𝅯	𝄿	$\frac{1}{4}$ × 𝅘𝅥

Dotted notes

• A dot after a note makes it longer by half its value.

Time name	Note	Equals	
dotted semibreve (dotted whole note)	𝅝.	𝅝 + 𝅗𝅥	𝅗𝅥 + 𝅗𝅥 + 𝅗𝅥
dotted minim (dotted half note)	𝅗𝅥.	𝅗𝅥 + 𝅘𝅥	𝅘𝅥 + 𝅘𝅥 + 𝅘𝅥
dotted crotchet (dotted quarter note)	𝅘𝅥.	𝅘𝅥 + 𝅘𝅥𝅮	𝅘𝅥𝅮 + 𝅘𝅥𝅮 + 𝅘𝅥𝅮
dotted quaver (dotted 8th note)	𝅘𝅥𝅮.	𝅘𝅥𝅮 + 𝅘𝅥𝅯	𝅘𝅥𝅯 + 𝅘𝅥𝅯 + 𝅘𝅥𝅯

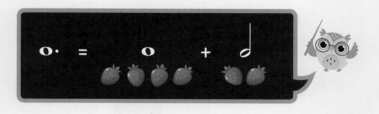

1 Write the notes and rests.

Time name	crotchet (quarter note)	quaver (8th note)	semibreve (whole note)	minim (half note)	semiquaver (16th note)
Note					
Rest					

2 Write the correct number.

(a) ♪ = [ ] ♫

(b) ♪. = [ ] ♫

(c) ♩ = [ ] ♪ = [ ] ♫

(d) ♩. = [ ] ♪ = [ ] ♫

(e) ♩ = [ ] ♩ = [ ] ♪ = [ ] ♫

(f) ♩. = [ ] ♩ = [ ] ♪ = [ ] ♫

(g) 𝅝 = [ ] ♩ = [ ] ♩ = [ ] ♪ = [ ] ♫

(h) 𝅝. = [ ] ♩ = [ ] ♩ = [ ] ♪ = [ ] ♫

3 Tick ✔ the correct number.

(a) **How many crotchets** (quarter notes) **are there in a semibreve** (whole note)?   4 [ ]   5 [ ]   6 [ ]   8 [ ]

(b) **How many semiquavers** (16th notes) **are there in a dotted minim** (dotted half note)?   4 [ ]   8 [ ]   12 [ ]   16 [ ]

(c) **How many quavers** (8th notes) **are there in a dotted semibreve** (dotted whole note)?   6 [ ]   8 [ ]   10 [ ]   12 [ ]

(d) **How many semiquavers** (16th notes) **are there in a dotted quaver** (dotted 8th note)?   3 [ ]   6 [ ]   9 [ ]   12 [ ]

Time signatures

• Each time signature has two numbers: $\frac{2}{4}$, $\frac{3}{4}$, $\frac{4}{4}$, and so on.

(a) The **top** number shows the number of beats in a bar.
(b) The **bottom** number shows the kind of beats in a bar.

> **Cut common time** (𝄵) is the same as $\frac{2}{2}$ time (also known as **alla breve**).

Simple duple	Simple triple	Simple quadruple
$\frac{2}{2}$ 1 2	$\frac{3}{2}$ 1 2 3	$\frac{4}{2}$ 1 2 3 4
2 minim beats (half note)	**3 minim** beats (half note)	**4 minim** beats (half note)
$\frac{2}{4}$ 1 2	$\frac{3}{4}$ 1 2 3	$\frac{4}{4}$ 1 2 3 4
2 crotchet beats (quarter note)	**3 crotchet** beats (quarter note)	**4 crotchet** beats (quarter note)
	$\frac{3}{8}$ 1 2 3	
	3 quaver beats (8th note)	

> **Common time** (𝄴) is the same as $\frac{4}{4}$ time.

4 Fill in notes. Complete the sentence.

(a) $\frac{2}{4}$ [♩ ♩] ‖ $\frac{2}{4}$ means _2 crotchet beats in a bar_

(b) $\frac{2}{2}$ ‖ $\frac{2}{2}$ means _____

(c) $\frac{3}{4}$ ‖ $\frac{3}{4}$ means _____

(d) $\frac{3}{2}$ ‖ $\frac{3}{2}$ means _____

(e) $\frac{4}{4}$ ‖ $\frac{4}{4}$ means _____

(f) $\frac{4}{2}$ ‖ $\frac{4}{2}$ means _____

(g) $\frac{3}{8}$ ‖ $\frac{3}{8}$ means _____

(h) 𝄵 ‖ 𝄵 means _____

5 Write the beats. Complete the time signature.

(a) **2** · ♩ ♩ | ♫ ♩ ‖
Beats: 1   2   1   2

(b) **3** · ♩. ♪ ♩ | ♩ ♩ ‖
Beats:

(c) **3** · ♩ ♩ ♩ ♩ | 𝅝. ‖
Beats:

(d) **4** · ♩ ♩ 𝅝 | ♩ ♩ ♩ 𝅝 ‖
Beats:

(e) **2** · ♩ ♩ | ♩ ♩ ♩ ‖
Beats:

(f) **3** · ♫♫ | ♩. ‖
Beats:

(g) **4** · ♩ ♩ ♩ ♩ | 𝅝 ‖
Beats:

(h) **2** · ♫♫ ♩ | 𝅝 ‖
Beats:

6 Circle the correct time signature. EXAM

❶ Identify beat type.
❷ Identify how many beats in each bar.

❶♪❷ 1   2   3   1   2   3

(a) $\frac{3}{8}$ $\frac{3}{4}$ $\frac{2}{4}$

(b) $\frac{4}{4}$ $\frac{4}{2}$ $\frac{2}{4}$

(c) $\frac{3}{2}$ $\frac{3}{4}$ C

(d) $\frac{3}{4}$ $\frac{3}{2}$ $\frac{2}{2}$

(e) $\frac{4}{2}$ $\frac{3}{2}$ $\frac{2}{2}$

(f) $\frac{3}{4}$ $\frac{2}{4}$ C

(g) $\frac{2}{4}$ ¢ $\frac{3}{4}$

Say with rhythm names and clap the rhythm.

7 Add the **one** missing bar-line. EXAM

❶ Identify beat type.
❷ Count beats.

Say with rhythm names and clap the rhythm.

Rewriting rhythms in different metres

8 Rewrite the notes or rests at **twice the value.**

(a)

(b)

1 Write notes/rests of twice the value.
2 Group and beam.

9 Rewrite the following using notes or rests of **twice the value.**

10 Rewrite the notes or rests at **half the value.**

(a)
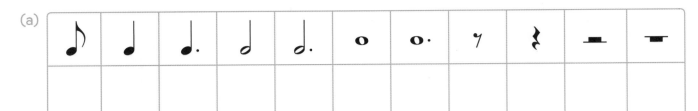

(b)
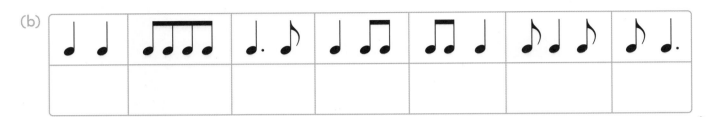

1 Write notes/rests of half the value.
2 Group and beam.

11 Rewrite the following using notes or rests of **half the value.**

(a)

(b)

12 Look at the given bar.
Tick ✔ the bar that is correctly rewritten using notes of **twice the value**.

(a)

(b)

(c)

(d)

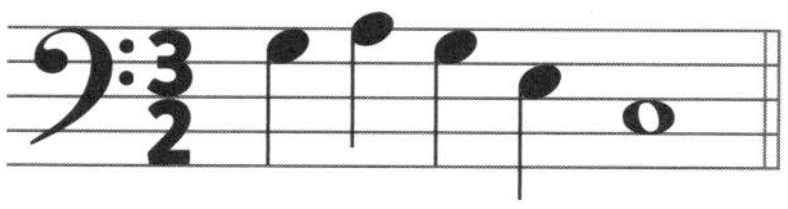

13 Look at the given bar.
Tick ✔ the bar that is correctly rewritten using notes of **half the value**.

Triplets
Grouping notes by beat
Grouping notes across multiple beats
Grouping rests

3 Rhythm 2

Triplets

• A triplet is a group of 3 notes played in the time of 2.

Triplet	Triplet with different note values	Triplet with rest(s)

Triplet over a beat

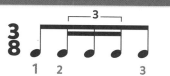

Triplet over half a beat

Triplet over multiple beats

Triplets can be grouped with regular notes.

1 Write a note that is equal to the triplet.

(a) are played in the time of two ☐

(b) are played in the time of two ☐

(c) are played in the time of a ☐

(d) are played in the time of a ☐

(e) are played in the time of two ☐

(f) are played in the time of a ☐

2 Write the correct number.

(a) How many <u>crotchets</u> (quarter notes) are equal to [notes] ?

(b) How many minims (half notes) are equal to [notes] ?

(c) How many quaver(s) (8th note) is/are equal to [notes] ?

(d) How many crotchets (quarter notes) are equal to [notes] ?

(e) How many quavers (8th notes) are equal to [notes] ?

3 Circle the correct time signature. EXAM

(a) [notation] $\frac{2}{4}$ $\frac{3}{4}$ $\frac{4}{4}$

(b) [notation] $\frac{2}{2}$ $\frac{4}{2}$ $\frac{3}{2}$

(c) [notation] $\frac{2}{4}$ $\frac{3}{4}$ 𝄴

(d) [notation] $\frac{2}{4}$ $\frac{2}{2}$ 𝄴

(e) [notation] $\frac{2}{2}$ $\frac{3}{2}$ $\frac{4}{2}$

(f) [notation] $\frac{2}{2}$ $\frac{3}{2}$ $\frac{4}{2}$

(g) [notation] $\frac{2}{4}$ $\frac{3}{4}$ $\frac{4}{4}$

(h) [notation] $\frac{3}{8}$ $\frac{2}{4}$ $\frac{3}{4}$

4 Add the **one** missing bar-line.

(a)

(b)

(c)

(d)

(e)

(f)

(g)

(h)

(i)

Grouping notes by beat

Crotchet (quarter note) beat

• In $\frac{2}{4}$, $\frac{3}{4}$ and $\frac{4}{4}$, beam notes in crotchet (quarter note) beats.

Minim (half note) beat

• In $\frac{2}{2}$, $\frac{3}{2}$ and $\frac{4}{2}$, beam notes in minim (half note) beats.

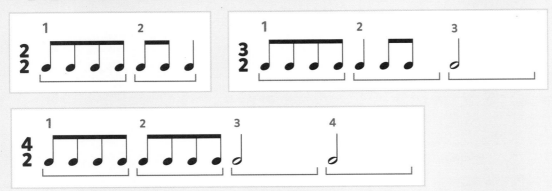

① Group beats.
② Beam notes.

5 Group the notes correctly.

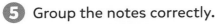

Grouping notes across multiple beats

- In $\frac{2}{4}$, beam notes across strong-weak beats (1-2).

- In $\frac{3}{4}$, beam notes across:-
  (a) strong-weak beats (1-2) (b) weak-weak beats (2-3)

- In $\frac{4}{4}$, beam notes across strong-weak beats (1-2, 3-4).

DO NOT beam from a weak to a strong beat

- In $\frac{3}{8}$, beam notes across strong-weak-weak beats (1-2-3).

- Avoid using ties within a bar when a single note could be used instead.

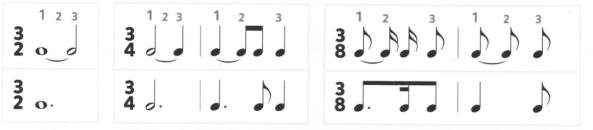

6 Tick ☑ the bar that is grouped correctly. [EXAM]

> 1 Identify beat type.
> 2 Identify how many beats in each bar.
> 3 Group beats.

Grouping rests

- Use a semibreve (whole note) rest for a complete bar of silence.

- Use a rest for each beat.

Minim beat (half note beat)	Crotchet beat (quarter note beat)	Quaver beat (8th note beat)

		DO NOT have a single rest from a weak to a strong beat.

- In $\frac{4}{2}$ and $\frac{4}{4}$, use a two-beat rest for beats 1-2 or 3-4.

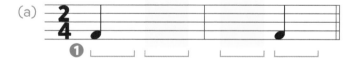

7 Add the correct rest(s) in each box.

① Mark out beats with brackets.

(a)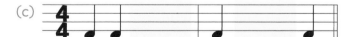

(b)

(c)

(d)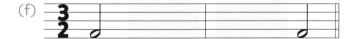

(e)

(f)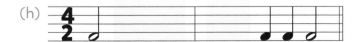

(g)

(h)

• Use a new rest for each subdivision of the beat.

Minim beat (half note beat)	Crotchet beat (quarter note beat)	Quaver beat (8th note beat)

8 Add the correct rest(s) in each box.

(a)

(b)

(c)

(d)

(e)

(f)

(g)

(h)

(i)

(j)

(k)

(l)

(m)

(n)

(o)

(p)

9 Tick ☑ or cross ☒ if the rests are correct **or** incorrect.

❶ Identify beat type.
❷ Write rest values.

The major scales of A, B♭ and E♭
Circle of 5ths: Major keys
Relative majors and minors
The minor scales of A, E and D

④ Keys and Scales

The major scales of A, B♭ and E♭

① Name the notes that make up the scale of **A major**.

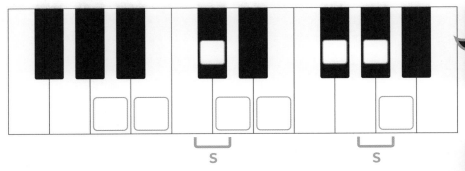

To make the scale of A major, C, F and G are raised a semitone to C♯, F♯ and G♯.

Two pairs of semitones: 3-4 and 7-8

② Add the accidental(s) needed to make the scale of **A major**.
Write the scale degrees. Mark the two pairs of notes that are a semitone apart.

A major, ascending

(a)
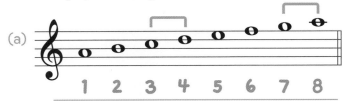
1 2 3 4 5 6 7 8

A major, descending

(b)
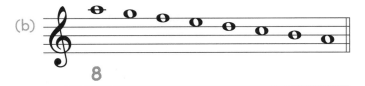
8

(c)
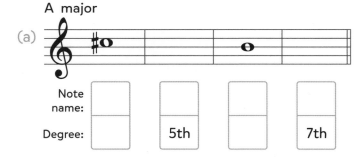

(d)
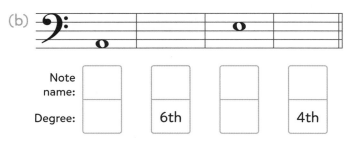

③ Write the notes, note names and scale degrees. Add any necessary accidental(s).

A major

(a)
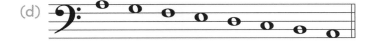

Note name: [ ] [ ] [ ] [ ]

Degree: [ ] 5th [ ] 7th

(b)

Note name: [ ] [ ] [ ] [ ]

Degree: [ ] 6th [ ] 4th

④ Copy the clef, key signature and key name.

(a)

A major _____

(b)

A major _____

5 Name the notes that make up the scale of **B♭ major**.

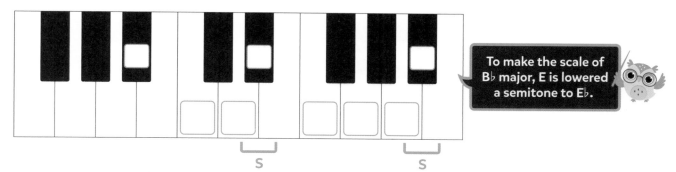

To make the scale of B♭ major, E is lowered a semitone to E♭.

6 Add the accidental(s) needed to make the scale of **B♭ major**. Write the scale degrees. Mark the two pairs of notes that are a semitone apart.

B♭ major, ascending

(a)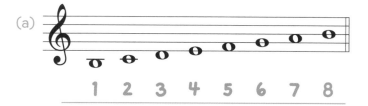

B♭ major, descending

(b)

(c)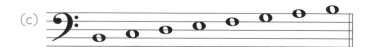

(d)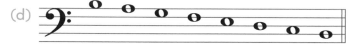

7 Write the notes, note names and scale degrees. Add any necessary accidental(s).

B♭ major

(a)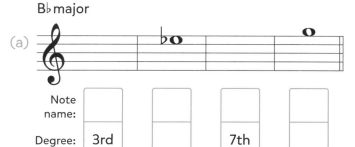

Note name:

Degree: | 3rd | | 7th |

(b)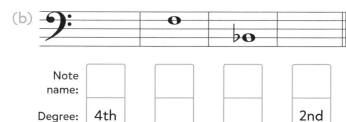

Note name:

Degree: | 4th | | | 2nd |

8 Copy the clef, key signature and key name.

(a)

B♭ major

(b)

B♭ major

9 Name the notes that make up the scale of E♭ major.

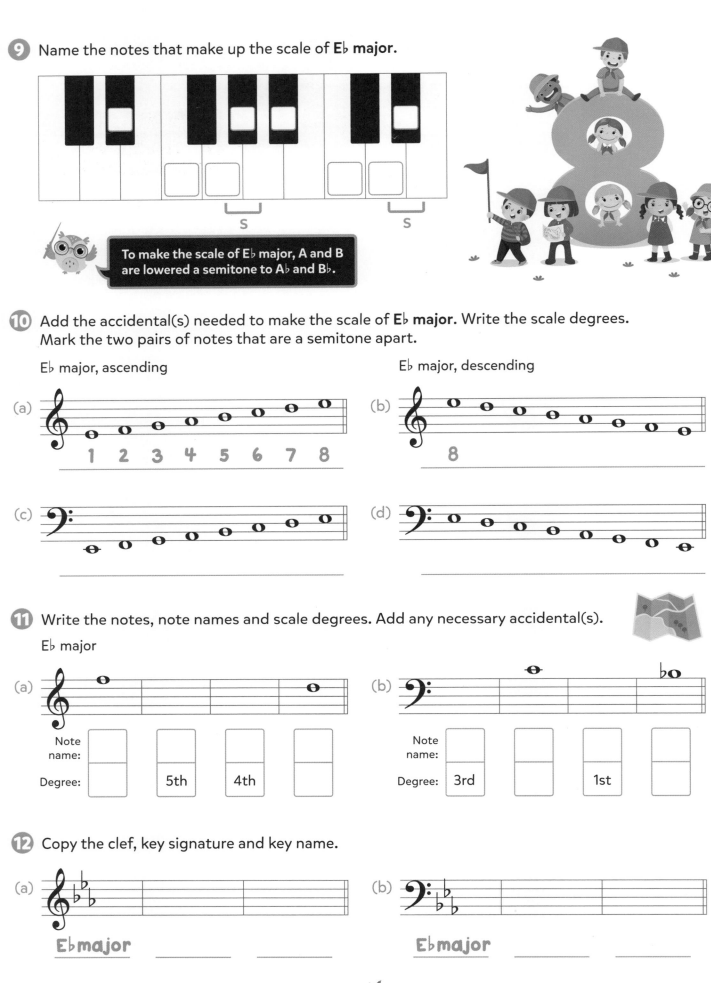

To make the scale of E♭ major, A and B are lowered a semitone to A♭ and B♭.

10 Add the accidental(s) needed to make the scale of E♭ major. Write the scale degrees. Mark the two pairs of notes that are a semitone apart.

E♭ major, ascending

(a)

1 2 3 4 5 6 7 8

E♭ major, descending

(b)

8

(c)

(d)

11 Write the notes, note names and scale degrees. Add any necessary accidental(s).

E♭ major

(a)

Note name:

Degree: 5th   4th

(b)

Note name:

Degree: 3rd   1st

12 Copy the clef, key signature and key name.

(a) E♭ major

(b) E♭ major

Circle of 5ths: Major keys

- To find major key signatures, count up/down to the next key, starting from C major (no sharps/flats).

  (a) Moving up in 5ths, each key signature adds a sharp.
  (b) Moving down in 5ths, each key signature adds a flat.

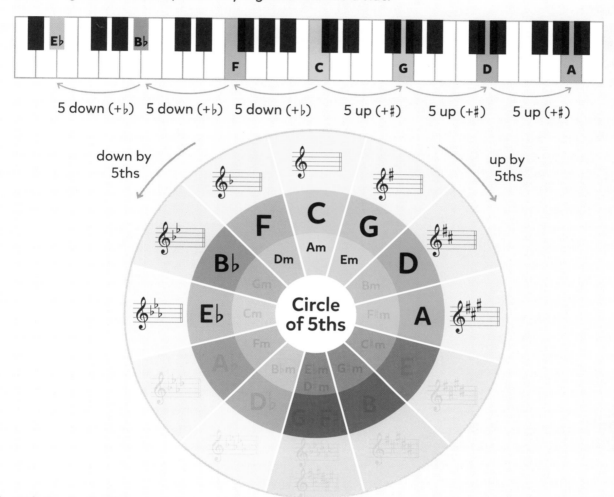

5 down (+♭) 5 down (+♭) 5 down (+♭) 5 up (+♯) 5 up (+♯) 5 up (+♯)

down by 5ths

up by 5ths

Circle of 5ths

Identifying major keys

In a flat key signature of two or more flats, the major key is the second last flat.

- Second last flat = E♭; key = E♭ major

In a sharp key signature, the major key is the note a semitone above the last (or only) sharp.

- Last sharp = G♯; key = A major (a semitone higher than G♯)

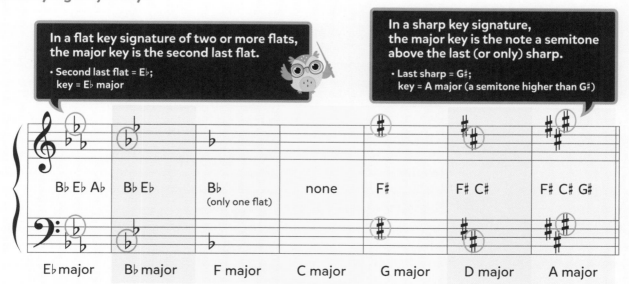

B♭ E♭ A♭	B♭ E♭	B♭ (only one flat)	none	F♯	F♯ C♯	F♯ C♯ G♯
E♭ major	B♭ major	F major	C major	G major	D major	A major

13 Name the key.

❶ For sharp keys, circle last (or only) sharp and name note a semitone higher.
❷ For flat keys, circle second last flat (if present) and name flat.

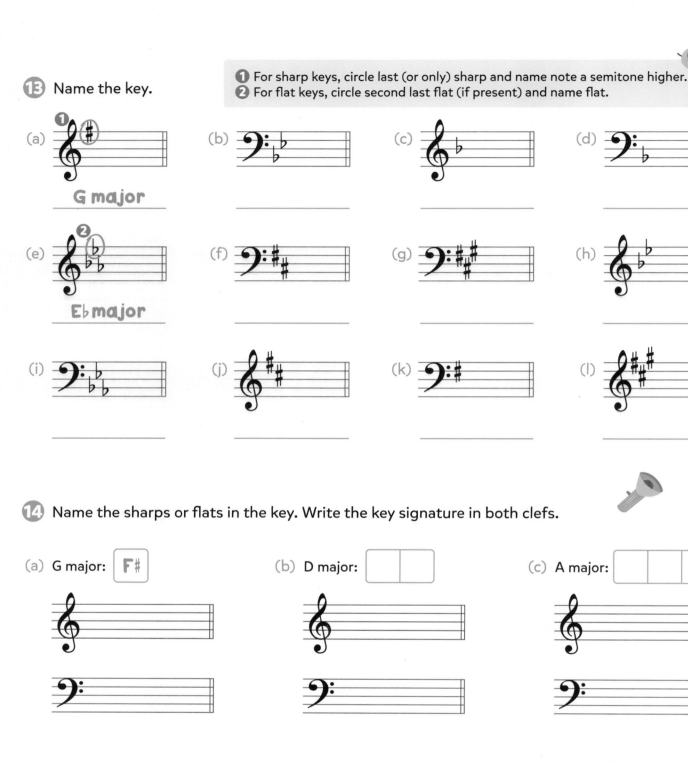

(a) ❶ G major

(b) _____

(c) _____

(d) _____

(e) ❷ E♭ major

(f) _____

(g) _____

(h) _____

(i) _____

(j) _____

(k) _____

(l) _____

14 Name the sharps or flats in the key. Write the key signature in both clefs.

(a) G major: [F♯]

(b) D major: [|]

(c) A major: [| |]

(d) F major: [ ]

(e) B♭ major: [|]

(f) E♭ major: [| |]

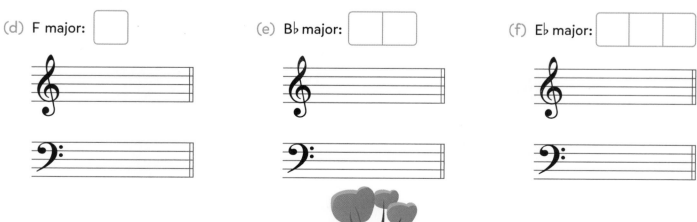

15 Write the scale in <u>semibreves</u> ❶ (whole notes), using a <u>key signature</u>.

❶ Underline keywords.
❷ Name sharps/flats in key.
❸ Write key signature noting clef.
❹ Indicate if scale is ascending/descending.

(a) <u>D major</u> ❶ F♯ C♯ ❷ ❸
<u>ascending</u> → ❹

(b) B♭ major ascending

(c) E♭ major descending

(d) A major descending

16 Write the scale in semibreves (whole notes).
Do not use a key signature, but add any necessary accidentals.

(a) G major ascending

(b) A major descending

(c) E♭ major ascending

(d) B♭ major descending

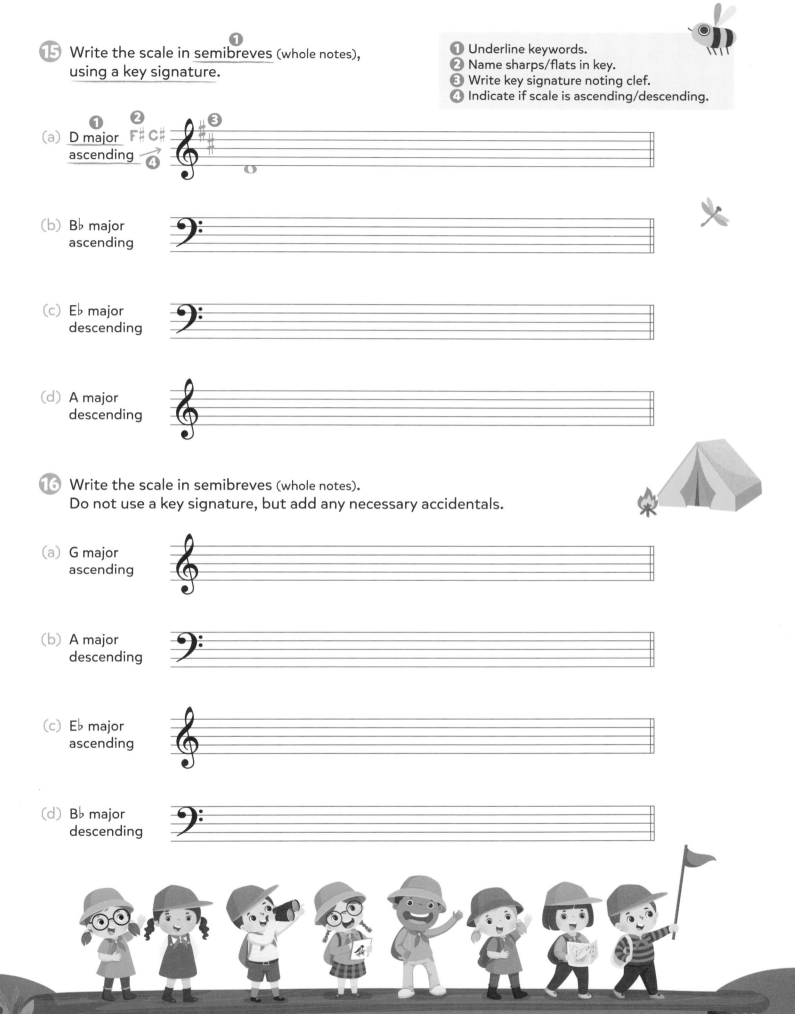

17 Tick ☑ the **three** notes that need an accidental to create a melody in the key.

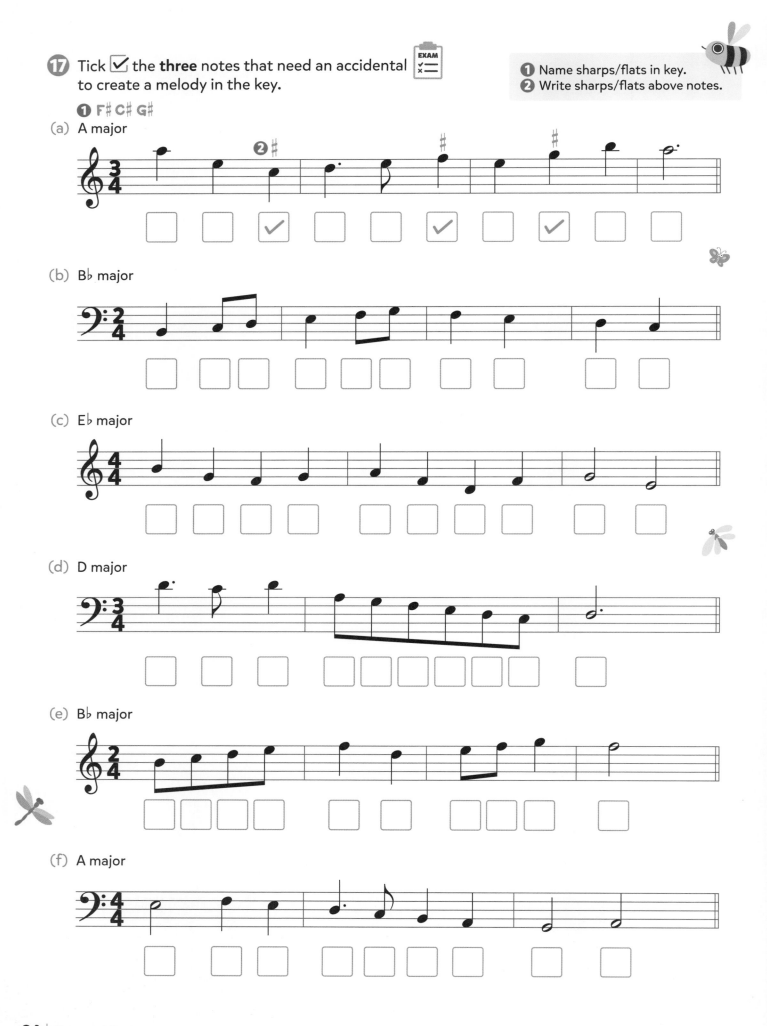

❶ Name sharps/flats in key.
❷ Write sharps/flats above notes.

❶ F♯ C♯ G♯

(a) A major

(b) B♭ major

(c) E♭ major

(d) D major

(e) B♭ major

(f) A major

18 Name the key.

1 Name each note with accidental.

(a)

_____ major

(b)

_____ major

(c)

_____ major

(d)

_____ major

19 Circle the correct key.

(a)

G major   B♭ major   E♭ major   F major

(b)

D major   A major   E♭ major   B♭ major

(c)

G major   D major   A major   F major

(d)

G major   D major   B♭ major   E♭ major

Relative majors and minors

- The relative minor of a major key (or the relative major of a minor key) has the same key signature but a different tonic.

  (a) To find the relative minor, count down 3 semitones from the major.
  (b) To find the relative major, count up 3 semitones from the minor.

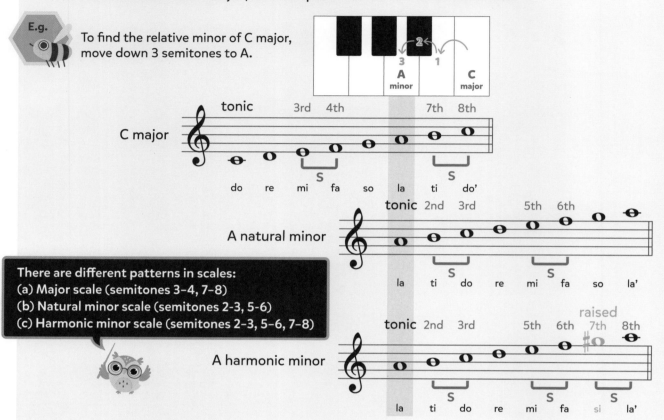

There are different patterns in scales:
(a) Major scale (semitones 3–4, 7–8)
(b) Natural minor scale (semitones 2–3, 5–6)
(c) Harmonic minor scale (semitones 2–3, 5–6, 7–8)

The minor scales of A, E and D

- The minor scales of A, E and D are derived from the major scales of C, G and F, respectively.

20 Find the relative minor key of the major key. Write the key signature.

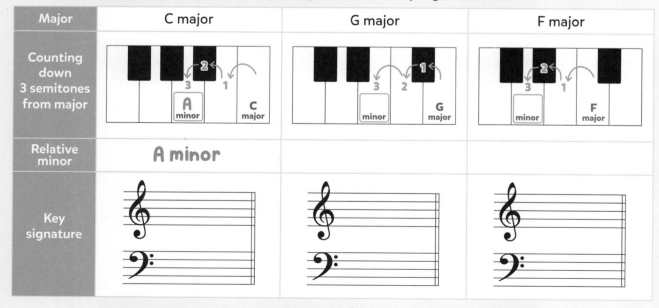

Major	C major	G major	F major
Counting down 3 semitones from major			
Relative minor	A minor		
Key signature			

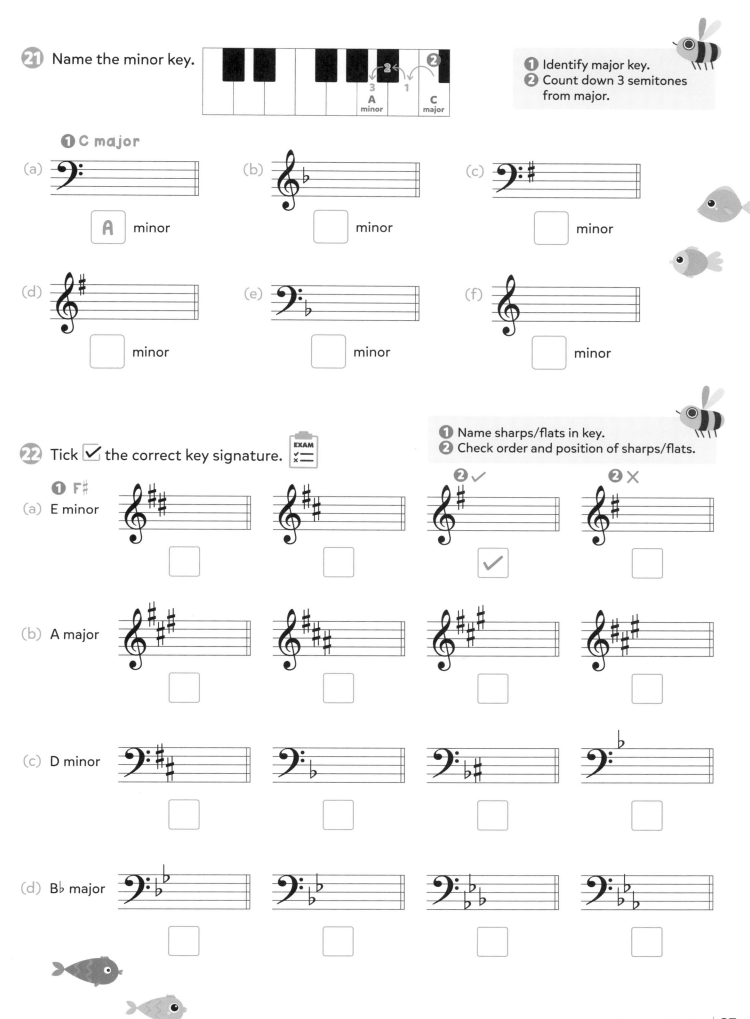

21 Name the minor key.

① Identify major key.
② Count down 3 semitones from major.

① C major

(a) A minor

(b) ___ minor

(c) ___ minor

(d) ___ minor

(e) ___ minor

(f) ___ minor

22 Tick ✓ the correct key signature. EXAM

① Name sharps/flats in key.
② Check order and position of sharps/flats.

① F♯

(a) E minor

② ✓   ② ✗

(b) A major

(c) D minor

(d) B♭ major

23 Name the notes that make up the minor scale. Add necessary sharps/flats and **raise the 7th degree.** Mark the three pairs of notes that are a semitone apart.

(a) A harmonic minor:

A			D	E		G#	
1st	2nd	3rd	4th	5th	6th	7th	8th

Semitones:
2-3, 5-6 and 7-8

ascending   descending

(b) E harmonic minor:

E							
1st	2nd	3rd	4th	5th	6th	7th	8th

ascending   descending

(c) D harmonic minor:

D							
1st	2nd	3rd	4th	5th	6th	7th	8th

ascending   descending

24 Circle the correct key for the melody. [EXAM]

1 Name notes with sharps/flats.
2 Identify major key.
3 Look for raised 7th in minor.

2 F major
1 B♭
3 C♯ (7th): D minor

(a) A minor (D minor) D major F major

(b) E minor C major A minor G major

(c) E minor D major A major A minor

(d) B♭ major D minor D major E♭ major

(e) G major E minor D major E♭ major

1 Underline keywords.
2 Name sharps/flats in key.
3 Write letter name for degree number.
4 Write letter name for note.
5 Verify statement.

25 Circle **TRUE** or **FALSE**. [EXAM]

4 G

(a) **3** G♯   **2** F♯ C♯ G♯   **5**
This is the 7th degree of the scale of A major   TRUE (FALSE)
1   **1**

(b) This is the 6th degree of the scale of E♭ major   TRUE FALSE

(c) This is the 3rd degree of the scale of D minor   TRUE FALSE

(d) This is the 4th degree of the scale of B♭ major   TRUE FALSE

(e) This is the 7th degree of the scale of E minor   TRUE FALSE

26 Tick ✔ the correct scale.

(a) E♭ major, ascending

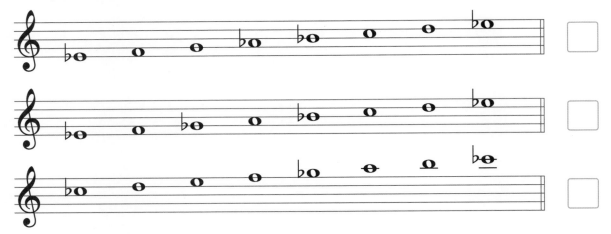

(b) B♭ major, descending

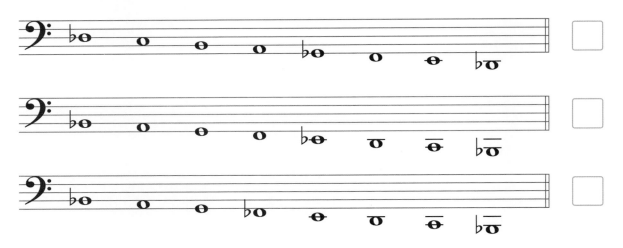

(c) A major, descending

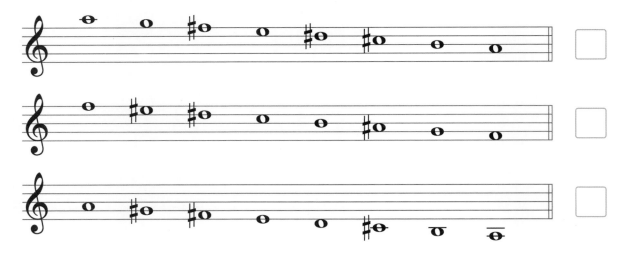

27 Tick ☑ the **two pairs** of notes that are a semitone apart.

❶ Write degrees above scale.
❷ Mark semitones (3-4, 7-8).

(28) Cross ☒ the **two** incorrect notes. 📋EXAM

① Name sharps/flats in key.
② Name raised 7th in minor key.
③ Write correct names above notes.

(a) D harmonic minor, ascending ① B♭ ② C♯   ③ B♭   C♯

☐ ☐ ☐ ☐ ☒ ☐ ☒

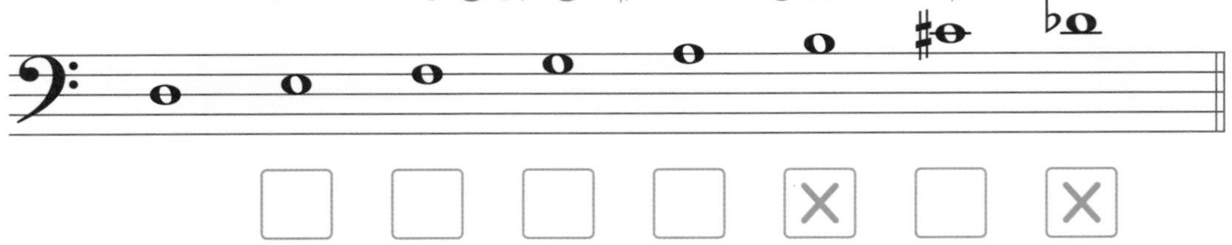

(b) A major, descending

☐ ☐ ☐ ☐ ☐ ☐ ☐

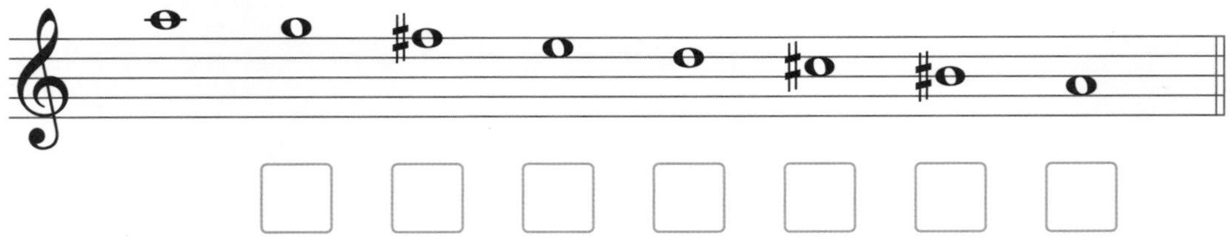

(c) D major, ascending

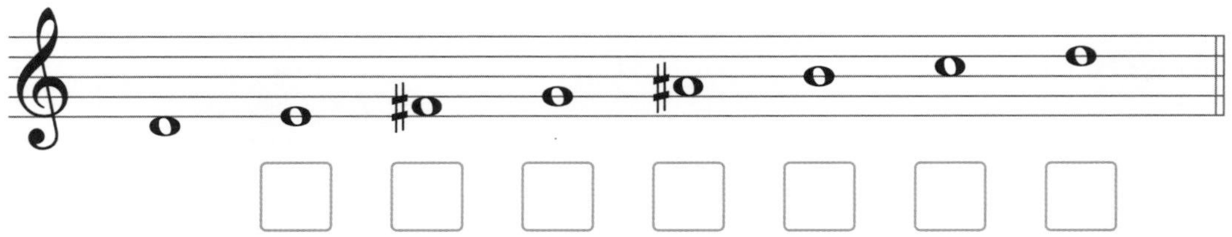

☐ ☐ ☐ ☐ ☐ ☐ ☐

(d) E♭ major, ascending

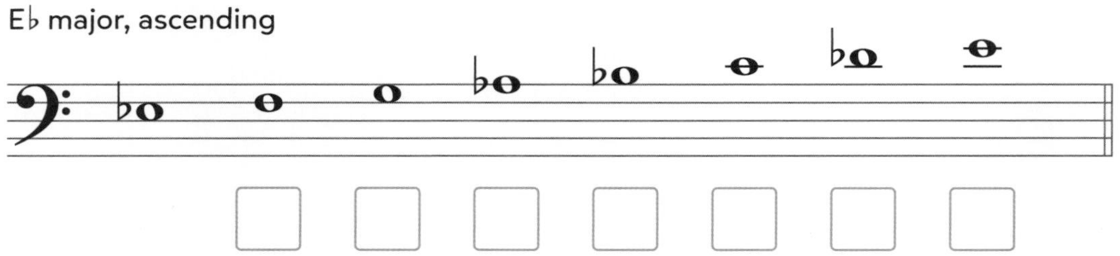

☐ ☐ ☐ ☐ ☐ ☐ ☐

(e) E harmonic minor, descending

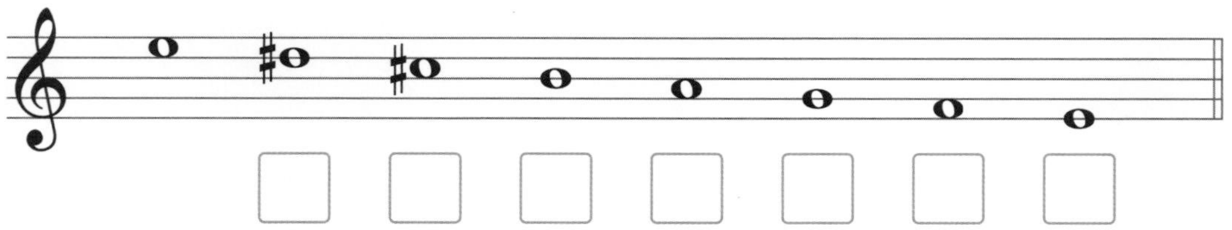

☐ ☐ ☐ ☐ ☐ ☐ ☐

29 Tick ✓ the **correct note for X and Y** and complete the scale. EXAM ☑

❶ Name sharps/flats in key.
❷ Write note for X and Y.

(a) A major ❶ **F♯ C♯ G♯**

X C ☐   C♯ ✓   E ☐   E♯ ☐   Y A ☐   A♯ ☐   G ☐   F♯ ✓

(b) A harmonic minor

X G ☐   G♯ ☐   E ☐   E♭ ☐   Y B ☐   B♭ ☐   D ☐   D♯ ☐

(c) E♭ major

X B ☐   B♭ ☐   G ☐   G♭ ☐   Y B ☐   B♭ ☐   D ☐   D♭ ☐

(d) D harmonic minor

X A ☐   C♯ ☐   C ☐   A♯ ☐   Y C ☐   C♯ ☐   E ☐   E♯ ☐

(e) B♭ major

X G ☐   E♭ ☐   E ☐   G♭ ☐   Y B ☐   G♭ ☐   G ☐   B♭ ☐

5 Intervals

Intervals in major and minor scales

• To identify an interval, count up the degrees from the tonic.

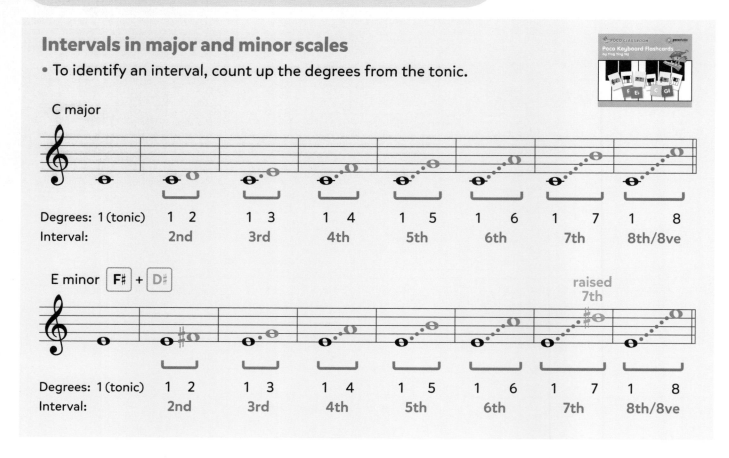

C major

Degrees:	1 (tonic)	1 2	1 3	1 4	1 5	1 6	1 7	1 8
Interval:		2nd	3rd	4th	5th	6th	7th	8th/8ve

E minor F♯ + D♯

raised 7th

Degrees:	1 (tonic)	1 2	1 3	1 4	1 5	1 6	1 7	1 8
Interval:		2nd	3rd	4th	5th	6th	7th	8th/8ve

---

1 Name the sharp(s) or flat(s) in the key and a raised 7th note if in a minor key.
Write a **higher** note after the tonic to form the named interval.
Add any necessary accidental(s).

> In minor scales, the 7th note is raised one semitone.

(a) A minor +

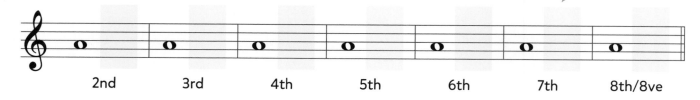

2nd   3rd   4th   5th   6th   7th   8th/8ve

(b) A major ☐ ☐ ☐

2nd   3rd   4th   5th   6th   7th   8th/8ve

(c) F major ☐

8th/8ve   6th   4th

5th   3rd   7th

(d) D minor ☐ + ☐

3rd   4th   7th

6th   5th   2nd

(e) G major ☐

6th   7th   5th

2nd   4th   3rd

(f) E minor ☐ + ☐

3rd   4th   7th

6th   5th   2nd

(g) D major ☐ ☐

4th   7th   3rd

6th   2nd   8th/8ve

(h) B♭ major

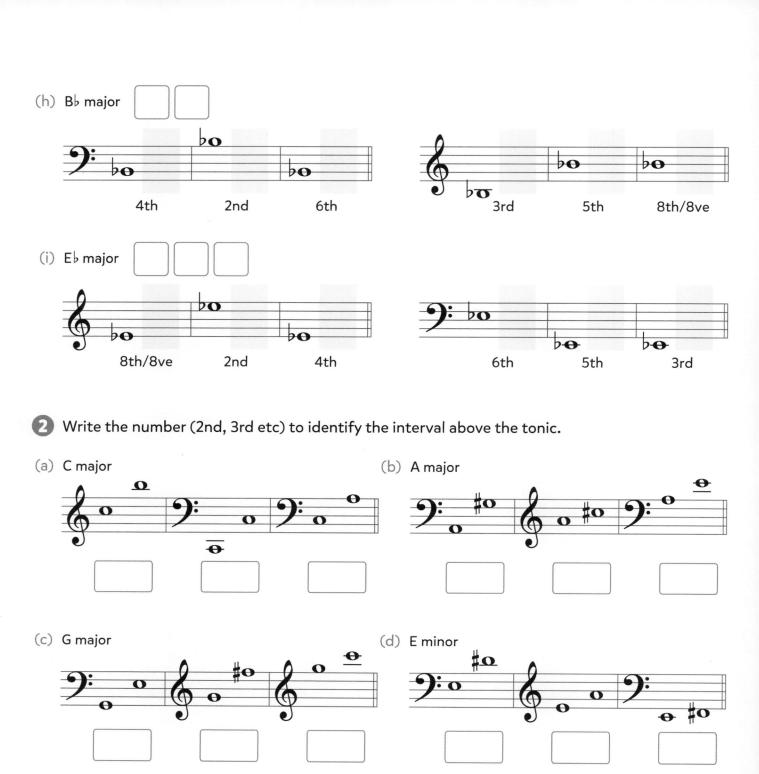

4th   2nd   6th   3rd   5th   8th/8ve

(i) E♭ major

8th/8ve   2nd   4th   6th   5th   3rd

2   Write the number (2nd, 3rd etc) to identify the interval above the tonic.

(a) C major   (b) A major

(c) G major   (d) E minor

(e) D major   (f) F major

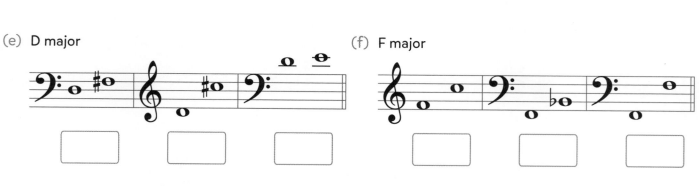

3 Tick ✓ the correct interval number.

(a)

2nd	3rd	4th	5th
☐	☐	☐	☐

(b)

5th	6th	7th	8th/8ve
☐	☐	☐	☐

(c)

4th	5th	6th	7th
☐	☐	☐	☐

(d)

1st	2nd	3rd	4th
☐	☐	☐	☐

(e)

3rd	4th	5th	6th
☐	☐	☐	☐

(f)

5th	6th	7th	8th/8ve
☐	☐	☐	☐

(g)

2nd	3rd	4th	5th
☐	☐	☐	☐

(h)

1st	2nd	3rd	4th
☐	☐	☐	☐

(i)

3rd	5th	6th	7th
☐	☐	☐	☐

(j)

3rd	5th	6th	8th/8ve
☐	☐	☐	☐

(k)

4th	5th	7th	8th/8ve
☐	☐	☐	☐

(l)

2nd	3rd	6th	8th/8ve
☐	☐	☐	☐

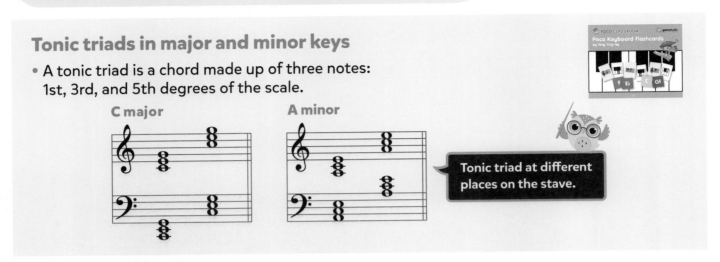

6 Tonic Triads

Tonic triads in major and minor keys

- A tonic triad is a chord made up of three notes: 1st, 3rd, and 5th degrees of the scale.

C major   **A minor**

Tonic triad at different places on the stave.

1 Trace the key signatures and tonic triads.

	Sharp key			Flat key	
Key	**With key signature**	**Without key signature**	**Key**	**With key signature**	**Without key signature**
G major			F major		
E minor			D minor		
D major			B♭ major		
A major			E♭ major		

2 Name the notes and key of the tonic triad.

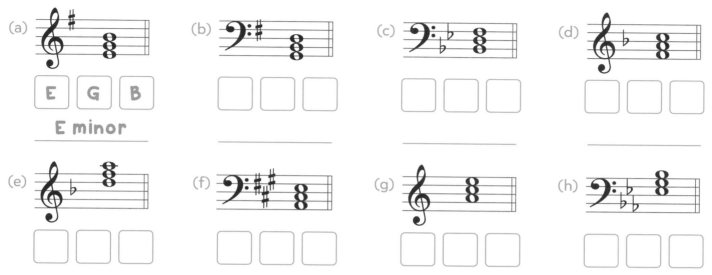

(a)

| E | G | B |

E minor

(b)

| | | |

(c)

| | | |

(d)

| | | |

(e)

| | | |

(f)

| | | |

(g)

| | | |

(h)

| | | |

3 Circle the correct key for the tonic triad. [EXAM]

① Name notes of triad.

(a)   C major   D minor   F major   D major

(b)   F major   B♭ major   E♭ major   D minor

(c)   E♭ major   F major   B♭ major   D minor

(d)   D major   D minor   F major   G major

(e)   A major   A minor   E minor   F major

(f)   C major   G major   A major   A minor

(g)   D major   A major   F major   A minor

(h)   G major   D major   E minor   E♭ major

4 Circle **TRUE** or **FALSE**.

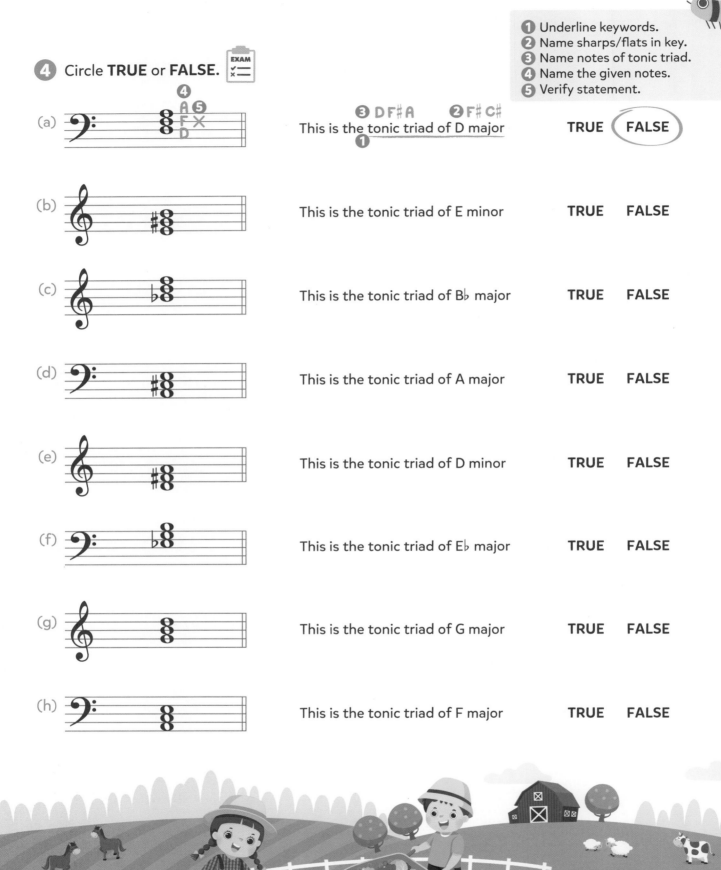

❶ Underline keywords.
❷ Name sharps/flats in key.
❸ Name notes of tonic triad.
❹ Name the given notes.
❺ Verify statement.

(a) ❸ D F♯ A   ❷ F♯ C♯
This is the tonic triad of D major   TRUE   ~~FALSE~~

(b) This is the tonic triad of E minor   TRUE   FALSE

(c) This is the tonic triad of B♭ major   TRUE   FALSE

(d) This is the tonic triad of A major   TRUE   FALSE

(e) This is the tonic triad of D minor   TRUE   FALSE

(f) This is the tonic triad of E♭ major   TRUE   FALSE

(g) This is the tonic triad of G major   TRUE   FALSE

(h) This is the tonic triad of F major   TRUE   FALSE

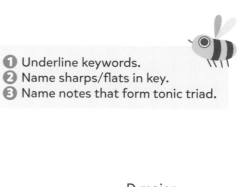

❶ Underline keywords.
❷ Name sharps/flats in key.
❸ Name notes that form tonic triad.

5 Add one note to complete the tonic triad ❶, with the tonic as the lowest note. Add any necessary accidental(s).

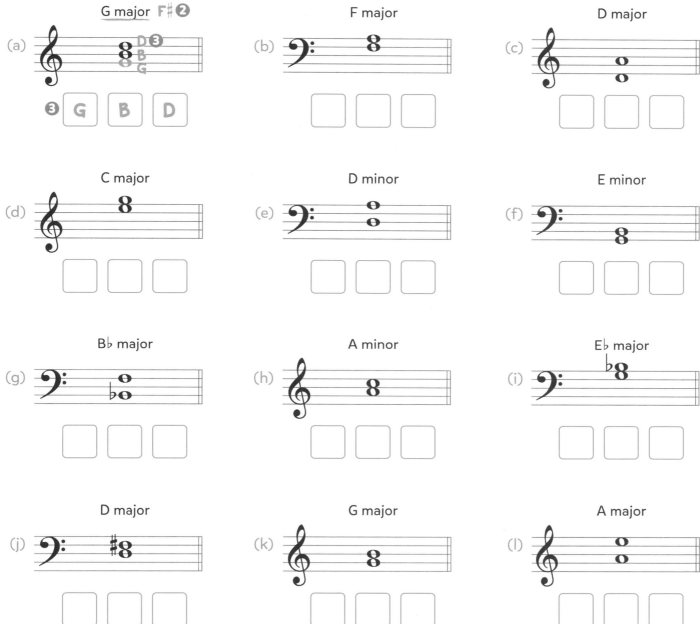

(a) G major F♯ ❷ — ❸ G B D

(b) F major

(c) D major

(d) C major

(e) D minor

(f) E minor

(g) B♭ major

(h) A minor

(i) E♭ major

(j) D major

(k) G major

(l) A major

Tempo

a tempo	in time (resume the original speed)
accelerando (accel.)	gradually getting quicker
Adagio	slow
Allargando	broadening
Allegretto	fair quick
Allegro	lively, quick
Andante	at a walking/ medium speed
con moto	with movement
Grave	very slow, solemn
rallentando (rall.)	gradually getting slower
ritardando (ritard., rit.)	gradually getting slower
Largo	slow, stately
Lento	slow
meno mosso	less movement
Moderato	at a moderate speed
più mosso	more movement
Presto	fast
ritenuto (*riten., rit.*)	getting slower, held back
Vivace, Vivo	lively, quick

Tempo

1 Tick ✔ the correct answer.

(a) What does **Largo** mean? ☐ sweet ☐ slow ☐ fast

(b) What does **meno mosso** mean? ☐ less movement ☐ more movement ☐ with movement

(c) What is the Italian word for 'broadening' ? ☐ **Allargando** ☐ **Alla marcia** ☐ **Allegro**

(d) Which is slower: **Vivace** or **Andante**? ☐ **Vivace** ☐ **Andante**

(e) Which is faster: **Grave** or **Lento**? ☐ **Grave** ☐ **Lento**

2 Give the correct meaning.

(a) **con moto** _____ (b) **Allargando** _____

(c) **Grave** _____ (d) **Lento** _____

(e) **Largo** _____ (f) **Presto** _____

(g) **meno mosso** _____ (h) **più mosso** _____

(i) **Vivace** _____ (j) **ritenuto** _____

3 Match each term to the correct meaning.

Adagio

Largo

Moderato

Allegretto

Vivace

Allegro

Lento

Grave

Andante

Presto

very slow

slow

moderate

at a walking speed

fairly quick

lively, quick

fast

Dynamics

⟍ crescendo (cresc.)	gradually getting louder
⟋ decrescendo (decresc.) diminuendo (dim.)	gradually getting quieter
f (forte)	loud
ff (fortissimo)	very loud
fp (fortepiano)	loud, then immediately quiet
mf (mezzo forte)	moderately loud (mezzo: half)
mp (mezzo piano)	moderately quiet
p (piano)	quiet
pp (pianissimo)	very quiet

Expression

cantabile	in a singing style
dolce	sweet
alla marcia	in the style of a march
espressivo (espress.)	expressive
grazioso	graceful

General

con, col	with	*senza*	without
meno	less	*più*	more
poco	a little	*molto*	very, much
e, ed	and	*non troppo*	not too much
ma	but	*poco a poco*	little by little

Dynamics

4 Tick ✓ the correct answer. [EXAM]

(a) **pp** means:
- [ ] quiet
- [ ] very quiet
- [ ] very loud
- [ ] moderately quiet

(b) **mp** means:
- [ ] loud
- [ ] very quiet
- [ ] moderately quiet
- [ ] quiet

(c) **dim.** means:
- [ ] gradually getting quicker
- [ ] gradually getting quieter
- [ ] gradually getting slower
- [ ] gradually getting louder

(d) **mf** means:
- [ ] loud
- [ ] very loud
- [ ] moderately quiet
- [ ] moderately loud

(e) **fp** means:
- [ ] loud, then immediately quiet
- [ ] quiet, then immediately loud
- [ ] forced, accented
- [ ] loud, gradually getting quieter

(f) **cresc.** means:
- [ ] gradually getting slower
- [ ] gradually getting quicker
- [ ] gradually getting louder
- [ ] gradually getting quieter

Expression & General

5 Give the correct meaning.

(a) *dolce* _____

(b) *grazioso* _____

(c) *espressivo (espress.)* _____

(d) *cantabile* _____

(e) *alla marcia* _____

(f) *senza* _____

(g) *poco* _____

(h) *molto* _____

(i) *più* _____

(j) *con* _____

(k) *meno* _____

(l) *non troppo* _____

(m) *poco a poco* _____

(n) *presto, ma non troppo* _____

(o) *moderato alla marcia* _____

(p) *molto vivace* _____

Articulation

	**slur**: perform the notes smoothly
	tie: perform the 1st note and hold for the value of both notes
legato	smoothly

6 Fill in the boxes with the correct letters.

	staccato: detached	
	staccatissimo: very detached	
	portato: slightly separated	
	accent the note: play the note with emphasis	
	strong accent/marcato: play the note with strong emphasis	
	tenuto: give the note slight pressure	

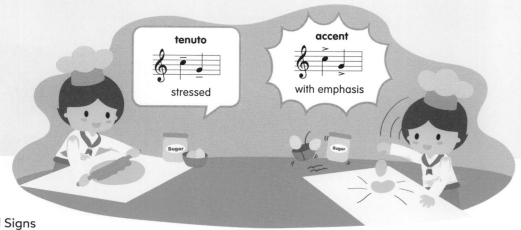

tenuto
stressed

accent
with emphasis

Musical Signs

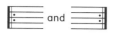 and   repeat the section between the two signs

 = 88   88 crotchet (quarter note) beats in a minute

pause on the note or rest

da capo (D.C)   repeat from the beginning

Fine   the end (*al Fine*: to the end)

dal segno (D.S)   repeat from the sign 𝄋

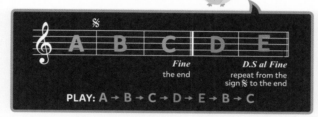

PLAY: A → B → C → D → E → B → C

7 Fill in the boxes with the correct letters.

8va - - - - - ⌐   perform an octave higher

   rest for the number of bars indicated

| 1 ⌐   first ending: when there's a repeat sign, play this section first time through only

| 2 ⌐   second ending: play bar(s) second time through

8 Write in the **terms** or **signs** to match the meanings.

(a) Show how this music should be played.

- in a marching style
- moderately loud
- with accent marks on minims (half notes)
- gradually getting louder at bar 3

(b) Show how this music should be played.

- slowly
- with a pause on the last note
- in a singing style
- moderately quiet

(c) Show how this music should be played.

- at a medium (walking) speed
- with tenuto marks on crotchets (quarter notes)
- expressively
- an octave higher than written

(d) Show how this music should be played.

- gracefully
- quietly
- gradually getting slower at bar 3
- with a pause on the last note

 Say with rhythm names and clap the rhythm.

(e) Show how this music should be played.

- sweetly
- moderately quiet
- with staccato marks on crotchets (quarter notes)
- an octave higher than written

(f) Show how this music should be played.

- lively and quick
- loudly
- with tenuto marks on crotchets (quarter notes)
- with a pause on the last note

 Say with rhythm names and clap the rhythm.

Musical Terms

9 Tick ✓ the correct answer.

(a) **accelerando** means:

- [ ] gradually getting quieter
- [ ] gradually getting louder
- [ ] gradually getting quicker
- [ ] gradually getting slower

(b) **Adagio** means:

- [ ] quick
- [ ] slow
- [ ] fairly quick
- [ ] gradually getting slower

(c) **Con moto** means:

- [ ] with movement
- [ ] more movement
- [ ] less movement
- [ ] without movement

(d) **allargando** means:

- [ ] very slow, solemn
- [ ] broadening
- [ ] slow, stately
- [ ] getting quicker

(e) **Allegretto** means:

- [ ] gradually getting slower
- [ ] slow
- [ ] fairly quick
- [ ] gradually getting quicker

(f) **rall.** means:

- [ ] slow
- [ ] gradually getting slower
- [ ] gradually getting quicker
- [ ] gradually getting louder

(g) **Allegro** means:

☐ fairly quick
☐ at a walking/medium speed
☐ quick
☐ slow

(h) **alla marcia** means:

☐ more movement
☐ not too much
☐ less movement
☐ in the style of a march

(i) **molto** means:

☐ a little
☐ in the style of
☐ very, much
☐ without

(j) **ritenuto** means:

☐ slow
☐ held back
☐ gradually getting slower
☐ gradually getting quieter

(k) **Presto** means:

☐ broadening
☐ fast
☐ at a walking/medium speed
☐ rather slow

(l) *grazioso* means:

☐ graceful
☐ sweet
☐ with movement
☐ majestic

(m) **Vivo** means:

☐ slow
☐ lively, quick
☐ at a walking/medium speed
☐ fairly quick

(n) **legato** means:

☐ more movement
☐ detached
☐ smoothly
☐ accent the note

Musical Signs

10 Tick ☑ the correct answer.

(a) ♩ means:

☐ strong accent
☐ *staccato*
☐ slight pressure
☐ *sforzando*

(b) ⌒ means:

☐ slur: perform the notes smoothly
☐ tie: detached
☐ slur: detached
☐ tie: perform the 1st note and hold for the value of both notes

(c) ♩♩♩ means:

- [ ] *staccato*
- [ ] slightly separated
- [ ] *staccatissimo*
- [ ] smoothly

(d) 8va ‒‒‒‒‒‒‒ means:

- [ ] perform an octave higher
- [ ] pause on the note or rest
- [ ] perform an octave lower
- [ ] perform the notes smoothly

(e) ♩ = 54 means:

- [ ] 54 crotchets (quarter notes) in a bar
- [ ] 54 crotchet (quarter note) beats in a minute
- [ ] 54 crotchets (quarter notes) in the melody
- [ ] 54 crotchet (quarter note) notes

(f) ♩ means:

- [ ] *staccato*: smoothly
- [ ] *staccato*: detached
- [ ] *legato*: detached
- [ ] *legato*: smoothly

(g) ♩ ♩ means:

- [ ] slightly separated
- [ ] slightly pressure
- [ ] *staccatissimo*
- [ ] *staccato*

(h) ◁ means:

- [ ] gradually getting quieter
- [ ] accent the note
- [ ] gradually getting louder
- [ ] loud

(i) ⌢ means:

- [ ] perform an octave higher
- [ ] *legato*: smoothly
- [ ] pause on the note or rest
- [ ] *staccato*: detached

(j) ▬▬2▬▬ means:

- [ ] 2 beats in a bar
- [ ] repeat the last 2 bars
- [ ] change to ²⁄₂ time
- [ ] rest for 2 bars

(k) **da capo (D.C)** means:

- [ ] repeat from the beginning
- [ ] in a singing style
- [ ] the end
- [ ] repeat from the sign 𝄋

(l) **dal segno (D.S)** means:

- [ ] repeat from the beginning
- [ ] in a singing style
- [ ] the end
- [ ] repeat from the sign 𝄋

8 Music in Context

Music in Context

- Music in Context relates all the elements of music to a complete melody and helps students to express the composer's intentions in performance.

1 Answer the questions based on the melody. [EXAM]

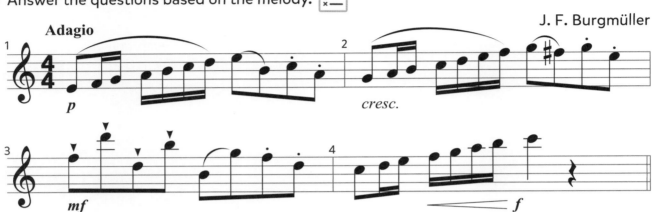

J. F. Burgmüller

1.1 Circle **TRUE** or **FALSE**.

(a) The melody gets gradually louder towards the end.   TRUE   FALSE

(b) The melody should be played fast.   TRUE   FALSE

(c) Bar 4 contains an ascending scale of C major.   TRUE   FALSE

1.2 Tick ☑ the correct number of times the rhythm ♪♫ occurs.

  2 ☐   3 ☐   4 ☐   5 ☐

1.3 Tick ☑ the correct answer.

(a) The **highest** note in the melody is a ...

  C ☐   D ☐   G ☐   B ☐

(b) There is a crotchet (quarter note) rest in ...

  bar 1 ☐   bar 2 ☐   bar 3 ☐   bar 4 ☐

(c) The letter name of the **longest** note in the melody is ...

  crotchet (quarter note) ☐   minim (half note) ☐   semibreve (whole note) ☐   quaver (8th note) ☐

2 Answer the questions based on the melody.

2.1 Circle **TRUE** or **FALSE**.

(a) The melody should be played gracefully.   TRUE   FALSE

(b) All the notes of tonic triad of G major can be found in bar 2.   TRUE   FALSE

2.2 Tick ☑ the correct number of triplets in the melody.

3 ☐   4 ☐   5 ☐   6 ☐

2.3 Tick ☑ the correct answer.

(a) Bar 1 has the same rhythm as ...

bar 3 ☐   bar 4 ☐   bar 5 ☐   bar 6 ☐

(b) The letter name of the **lowest** note in the melody is ...

G ☐   F ☐   F♯ ☐   A ☐

(c) How many times does the 2nd degree of the scale of G major occur?

4 ☐   6 ☐   8 ☐   10 ☐

3 Answer the questions based on the melody.

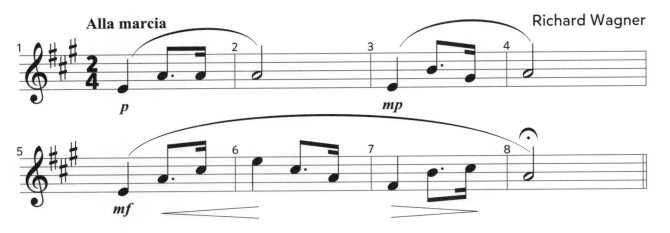

3.1 Circle **TRUE** or **FALSE**.

(a) The melody should be played in a singing style.   **TRUE   FALSE**

(b) The melody gets quieter towards the end.   **TRUE   FALSE**

3.2 Tick ☑ the correct number of times the rhythm  occurs.

2 ☐   3 ☐   4 ☐   5 ☐

3.3 Tick ☑ the correct answer.

(a) There is a pause on a note in ...

bar 3 ☐   bar 4 ☐   bar 6 ☐   bar 8 ☐

(b) The tonic triad of A major can be found in...

bar 3 ☐   bar 5 ☐   bar 6 ☐   bar 7 ☐

(c) The **loudest** bar in the melody is ...

bar 1 ☐   bar 4 ☐   bar 5 ☐   bar 6 ☐

4 Answer the questions based on the melody.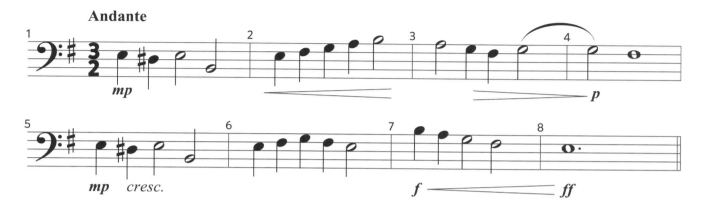

4.1 Circle **TRUE** or **FALSE**.

(a) $\frac{3}{2}$ means three crotchet (quarter note) beats in a bar. **TRUE   FALSE**

(b) All the notes in bars 1-4 of this melody can be found in the key of G major. **TRUE   FALSE**

4.2 Tick ☑ the bar with all the 3 notes of the tonic triad of E minor.

bar 1 ☐   bar 2 ☐   bar 3 ☐   bar 4 ☐

4.3 Tick ☑ the correct answer.

(a) The notes in bar 1 have the same pitch as ...

bar 3 ☐   bar 4 ☐   bar 5 ☐   bar 6 ☐

(b) The **loudest** note in the melody is in...

bar 4 ☐   bar 5 ☐   bar 7 ☐   bar 8 ☐

(c) The 7th degree of E minor scale can be found in ...

bar 2 ☐   bar 3 ☐   bar 4 ☐   bar 5 ☐

9

Model Test Paper

Total marks: /75

Exam duration: 1½ hours maximum

1 Rhythm

/15

1.1 Circle the correct time signature.

(3)

(a) $\frac{2}{4}$ $\frac{3}{8}$ $\frac{2}{2}$

(b) $\frac{4}{4}$ $\frac{3}{4}$ $\frac{2}{4}$

(c) $\frac{4}{2}$ 𝄴 $\frac{3}{2}$

1.2 Add the **one** missing bar-line.

(5)

(a)

(b)

(c)

(d)

(e)

1.3 Tick ✔ **one** box to answer the question. (2)

(a) How many quavers (8th notes) are equal to a dotted crotchet (dotted quarter note)?　　2 ☐　3 ☐　4 ☐　6 ☐

(b) How many semiquavers (16th notes) are equal to a dotted minim (dotted half note)?　　4 ☐　6 ☐　8 ☐　12 ☐

1.4 Tick ✔ **one** box to show the bar that is grouped correctly. (1)

☐　　　　☐　　　　☐

1.5 Tick ✔ **or** cross ✘ if the rests are correct **or** incorrect. (3)

☐　　　☐　　　☐

1.6 Look at this bar of music: (1)

Tick ✔ **one** box to show the bar that is correctly rewritten using notes of **twice the value**.

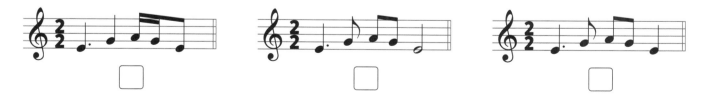

☐　　　　☐　　　　☐

2 Pitch

2.1 Tick ☑ **one** box to show the correct name. (6)

(a)

Bb	Eb	Db	Gb
☐	☐	☐	☐

(b)

B	Bb	Gb	G
☐	☐	☐	☐

(c)

G	B	D	G#
☐	☐	☐	☐

(d)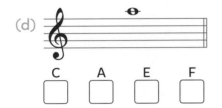

C	A	E	F
☐	☐	☐	☐

(e)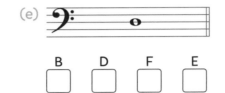

B	D	F	E
☐	☐	☐	☐

(f)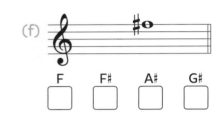

F	F#	A#	G#
☐	☐	☐	☐

2.2 Tick ☑ the correct clef. (2)

(a)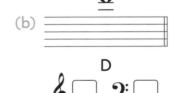

G

𝄞 ☐ 𝄢 ☐

(b)

D

𝄞 ☐ 𝄢 ☐

2.3 Rewrite the note at the same pitch in the new clef. (4)

(a)  (b)  (c)  (d)

2.4 Circle **TRUE** or **FALSE**. (3)

(a)  The first note sounds **higher** than the second note   **TRUE**   **FALSE**

(b)  The second note sounds **higher** than the first note   **TRUE**   **FALSE**

(c)  The first note sounds **lower** than the second note   **TRUE**   **FALSE**

3 Keys and Scales

3.1 Tick ☑ **one** box to show the correct key signature of B♭ major.   (1)

3.2 Tick ☑ **one** box to show the correct key signature of E minor.   (1)

3.3 Tick ☑ the **three** notes that need an accidental to create a melody in A major.   (3)

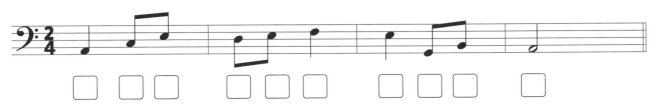

3.4 Circle the correct key.   (2)

(a)   E minor   D minor   G major   D major

(b)   D minor   E minor   B♭ major   F major

3.5 Circle **TRUE** or **FALSE**.   (1)

This is the 7th degree of the scale of D major   **TRUE**   **FALSE**

3.6 Tick ☑ **one** box to show the correct scale of E♭ major, descending. (1)

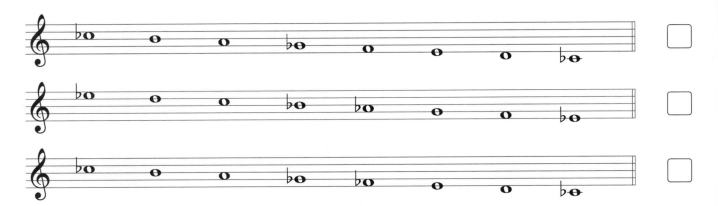

3.7 Tick ☑ the **two pairs** of notes that are a semitone apart. (2)

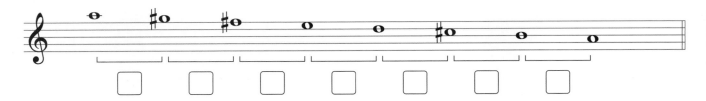

3.8 Cross ☒ the **two** incorrect notes.

D harmonic minor, ascending

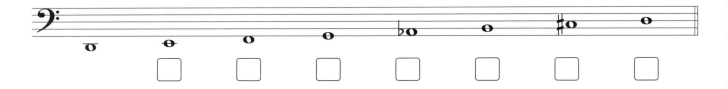

3.9 Tick ☑ **one note for X** and **one note for Y** to complete the scale of B♭ major. (2)

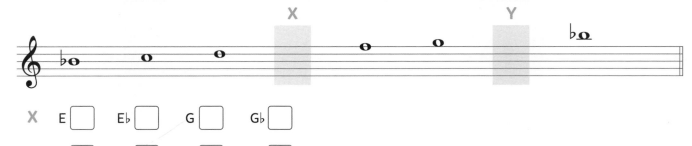

X   E ☐   E♭ ☐   G ☐   G♭ ☐

Y   C ☐   B ☐   A ☐   A♭ ☐

4 Intervals

Tick ✓ **one** box to show the correct interval number.

(a)

2nd	3rd	4th	5th
☐	☐	☐	☐

(b)

5th	6th	7th	8th/8ve
☐	☐	☐	☐

(c)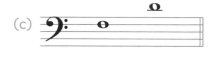

4th	5th	6th	7th
☐	☐	☐	☐

(d)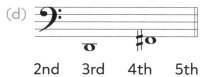

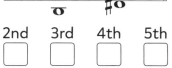

2nd	3rd	4th	5th
☐	☐	☐	☐

(e)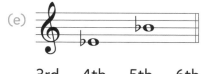

3rd	4th	5th	6th
☐	☐	☐	☐

(f)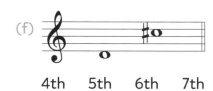

4th	5th	6th	7th
☐	☐	☐	☐

(g)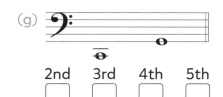

2nd	3rd	4th	5th
☐	☐	☐	☐

(h)

1st	2nd	3rd	4th
☐	☐	☐	☐

(i)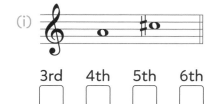

3rd	4th	5th	6th
☐	☐	☐	☐

(j)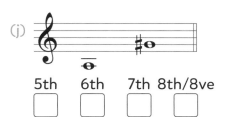

5th	6th	7th	8th/8ve
☐	☐	☐	☐

5 Tonic Triads

5.1 Circle **TRUE** or **FALSE**.

(2)

(a) 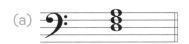   This is the tonic triad of D major   **TRUE**   **FALSE**

(b)    This is the tonic triad of A minor   **TRUE**   **FALSE**

5.2 Add **one** missing note to complete each tonic triad, with the tonic as the lowest note. Add any necessary accidental(s). (3)

(a) A major

(b) B♭ major

(c) E minor

5.3 Circle the correct key for each tonic triad. (5)

(a) E minor   D minor   D major   F major

(b) F major   G major   A major   D major

(c) A major   F major   A minor   C major

(d) E minor   G major   A major   E♭ major

(e) A major   D major   E minor   G major

6 Terms and Signs   /5

Tick ✓ **one** box for the term/sign. (5)

pp means:
quiet ☐
very loud ☐
very quiet ☐
loud ☐

cantabile means:
in time ☐
sweet ☐
slowly ☐
in a singing style ☐

legato means:
detached ☐
smoothly ☐
slow ☐
quiet ☐

alla marcia means:
in a singing style ☐
moderately ☐
more movement ☐
in the style of a march ☐

a tempo means:
the end ☐
in time ☐
slow ☐
in a singing style ☐

7 Music in Context

Answer the questions based on the melody.

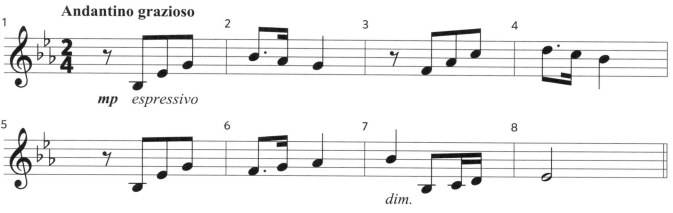

7.1 Circle **TRUE** or **FALSE**. (1)

The melody gets gradually louder towards the end. **TRUE**   **FALSE**

7.2 Tick ✔ the bar with all the notes of the tonic triad in E♭ major. (1)

bar 3 ☐   bar 5 ☐   bar 6 ☐   bar 7 ☐

7.3 Tick ✔ the correct answer. (3)

(a) The **shortest** note in the melody is a ...

crotchet ☐
(quarter note)

minim ☐
(half note)

semiquaver ☐
(16th note)

quaver ☐
(8th note)

(b) Bar 2 has the same rhythm as ...

bar 3 ☐   bar 4 ☐   bar 5 ☐   bar 7 ☐

(c) The letter name of the **lowest** note in the melody is ...

D ☐   G ☐   B ☐   B♭ ☐

⑩ Quick Revision

1 Rhythm

Time names and time values

Time Name	Note	Rest	Time Value	Note relationships
semibreve (whole note)	𝅝	▬	4 × ♩	𝅝
minim (half note)	𝅗𝅥	▬	2 × ♩	𝅗𝅥　　　　𝅗𝅥
crotchet (quarter note)	♩	𝄽	1 × ♩	♩　♩　♩　♩
quaver (8th note)	♪	𝄾	½ × ♩	♪ ♪ ♪ ♪ ♪ ♪ ♪ ♪
semiquaver (16th note)	𝅘𝅥𝅯	𝄿	¼ × ♩	𝅘𝅥𝅯 𝅘𝅥𝅯 𝅘𝅥𝅯 𝅘𝅥𝅯 𝅘𝅥𝅯 𝅘𝅥𝅯 𝅘𝅥𝅯 𝅘𝅥𝅯 𝅘𝅥𝅯 𝅘𝅥𝅯 𝅘𝅥𝅯 𝅘𝅥𝅯 𝅘𝅥𝅯 𝅘𝅥𝅯 𝅘𝅥𝅯 𝅘𝅥𝅯

- Use a semibreve (whole note) rest for a complete bar of silence.

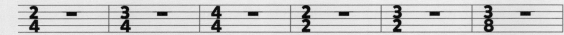

Dotted notes

Time name	Note	Equals	
dotted semibreve (dotted whole note)	𝅝·	𝅝 + 𝅗𝅥	𝅗𝅥 + 𝅗𝅥 + 𝅗𝅥
dotted minim (dotted half note)	𝅗𝅥·	𝅗𝅥 + ♩	♩ + ♩ + ♩
dotted crotchet (dotted quarter note)	♩·	♩ + ♪	♪ + ♪ + ♪
dotted quaver (dotted 8th note)	♪·	♪ + 𝅘𝅥𝅯	𝅘𝅥𝅯 + 𝅘𝅥𝅯 + 𝅘𝅥𝅯

Time signatures

Common time (𝄴) is the same as 4/4 time.
Cut common time (𝄵) is the same as 2/2 time (also known as **alla breve**).

Simple duple	Simple triple	Simple quadruple
2/2 𝅗𝅥 𝅗𝅥 (1 2)	**3/2** 𝅗𝅥 𝅗𝅥 𝅗𝅥 (1 2 3)	**4/2** 𝅗𝅥 𝅗𝅥 𝅗𝅥 𝅗𝅥 (1 2 3 4)
2 minim beats (half note)	**3 minim beats** (half note)	**4 minim beats** (half note)
2/4 ♩ ♩ (1 2)	**3/4** ♩ ♩ ♩ (1 2 3)	**4/4** ♩ ♩ ♩ ♩ (1 2 3 4)
2 crotchet beats (quarter note)	**3 crotchet beats** (quarter note)	**4 crotchet beats** (quarter note)
	3/8 ♪ ♪ ♪ (1 2 3)	
	3 quaver beats (8th note)	

Rewriting rhythms in different metres

Triplets

Triplet	Triplet with different note values	Triplet with rest(s)

Triplet over a beat	Triplet over half a beat	Triplet over multiple beats

Grouping notes by beat

Crotchet (quarter note) beat

• In $\frac{2}{4}$, $\frac{3}{4}$ and $\frac{4}{4}$, beam notes in crotchet (quarter note) beats.

Minim (half note) beat

• In $\frac{2}{2}$, $\frac{3}{2}$ and $\frac{4}{2}$, beam notes in minim (half note) beats.

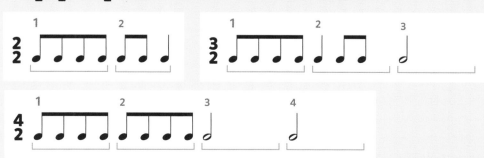

Grouping notes across multiple beats

- In $\frac{2}{4}$, beam notes across strong-weak beats (1-2).

- In $\frac{3}{4}$, beam notes across

(a) strong-weak beats (1-2)

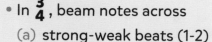

(b) weak-weak beats (2-3)

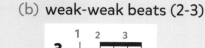

- In $\frac{4}{4}$, beam notes across strong-weak beats (1-2, 3-4).

DO NOT beam from a weak to a strong beat

- In $\frac{3}{8}$, beam notes across strong-weak-weak beats (1-2-3).

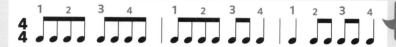

- Avoid using ties within a bar when a single note could be used instead.

Grouping rests

- Use a rest for each beat.

Minim beat (half note beat)	Crotchet beat (quarter note beat)	Quaver beat (8th note beat)
$\frac{2}{2}$	$\frac{2}{4}$	
$\frac{3}{2}$	$\frac{3}{4}$	$\frac{3}{8}$
$\frac{4}{2}$	$\frac{4}{4}$	DO NOT have a single rest from a weak to a strong beat.

- In $\frac{4}{2}$ and $\frac{4}{4}$, use a two-beat rest for beats 1-2 or 3-4.

• Use a new rest for each subdivision of the beat.

Minim beat (half note beat)	Crotchet beat (quarter note beat)	Quaver beat (8th note beat)
$\frac{2}{2}$ ♩ 𝄽 𝄽 ♩	$\frac{2}{4}$ ♪ 𝄾 𝄾 ♪	$\frac{3}{8}$ ♪ 𝄾 𝄾 ♪ ♪
$\frac{2}{2}$ ♩ 𝄽 𝄼	$\frac{2}{4}$ ♪ 𝄾 𝄽	$\frac{3}{8}$ ♪ 𝄾 𝄾 𝄾 ♪
$\frac{2}{2}$ ♪ 𝄾 𝄾 ♪ ♩	$\frac{2}{4}$ ♪ 𝄾 𝄾 ♪ ♪	$\frac{3}{8}$ ♪ 𝄾 𝄾 𝄾
$\frac{2}{2}$ ♪ 𝄾 𝄽 𝄼	$\frac{2}{4}$ ♪ 𝄾 𝄾 𝄽	$\frac{3}{8}$ 𝄾 𝄾 𝄾 ♪

2 Pitch

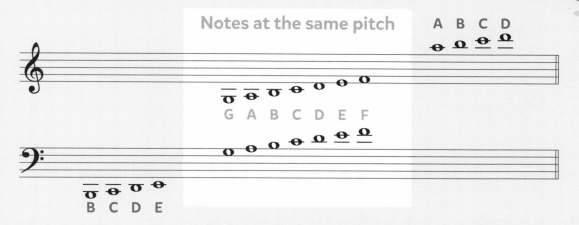

Notes at the same pitch

A B C D

G A B C D E F

B C D E

3 Keys and Scales

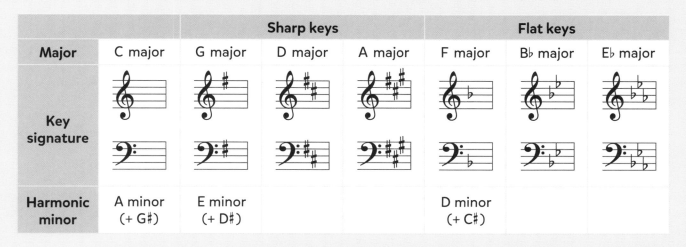

	Sharp keys				Flat keys		
Major	C major	G major	D major	A major	F major	B♭ major	E♭ major
Key signature							
Harmonic minor	A minor (+ G♯)	E minor (+ D♯)			D minor (+ C♯)		

4 Intervals

E minor F# + D#

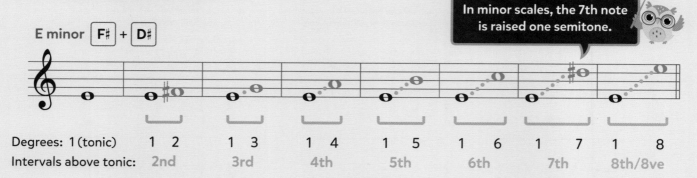

In minor scales, the 7th note is raised one semitone.

Degrees:	1 (tonic)	1 2	1 3	1 4	1 5	1 6	1 7	1 8
Intervals above tonic:		2nd	3rd	4th	5th	6th	7th	8th/8ve

5 Tonic Triads

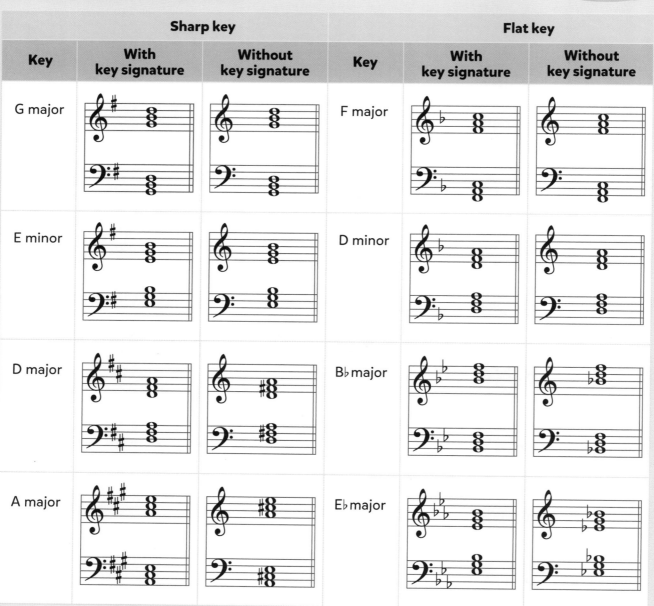

Sharp key			Flat key		
Key	With key signature	Without key signature	Key	With key signature	Without key signature
G major			F major		
E minor			D minor		
D major			Bb major		
A major			Eb major		

Meet the Author

Ying Ying Ng is author and co-founder of Poco Studio, an educational music publisher. Ying graduated from TU Dublin Conservatoire, majoring in music teaching for children. Through this life changing experience, she inherited a lifelong passion to teach music. For her lessons, Ying used to create teaching and learning materials to add to existing curricula since they were limited to textbooks and syllabuses, and inaccessible to students. All her books evolved through the many interactive exercises, visual aids, and game activities she painstakingly developed for her students. Ying authored several book series for Poco Studio, including *Music Theory for Young Children, Poco Piano for Young Children* (with Margaret O'Sullivan Farrell), *Sight Reading for Young Pianists, Music Theory for Young Musicians, Theory Drills for Young Children*, and *Poco Classroom Board Games*; these titles are well received by both students and teachers, with two series translated into Spanish and Simplified Chinese. She co-authored "*Teacher Handbook for Kodály's 333 Reading Exercises*" with Sarolta Platthy, and co-developed a Kodály-inspired music programme "*Every Child Sings*" with Borbála Szirányi and Alethia Bei Er Ngo.

Acknowledgements

I would like to acknowledge the debt of gratitude I owe to the students and teachers who used and have been using my books, as well as those who attended my seminars and workshops in Malaysia (since 2006), Singapore (2019), Indonesia (since 2006), Thailand (2012), China (2019), Hong Kong (2012), Taiwan (2014, 2019), and Australia (2021), for their feedback and motivation.

I wish to express my sincere gratitude and appreciation to those who gave me thorough and constructive comments on this and previous editions, including Margaret O'Sullivan Farrell, Dr Ita Beausang, Hiew Yee Ling, Wah Yi Shuen, and Wong Yee Ling.

I want to thank my husband cum copyeditor, Professor David Chek Ling Ngo, for being my source of inspiration to keep improving the content, and challenge how a layman understands the meaning of music.

And, to my two lovely daughters, Alethia Bei Er Ngo and Natasha Xue Er Ngo, who put up with me throughout the process of writing my books, many thanks. Alethia reviewed the early drafts with meticulous care.

Notes